POEMS AND STORIES

OF A

SALTGRASS COWBOY

BY

BOB KAHLA

To my lovely wife, Evette.

Front & Back cover by my friend, talented cowboy artist
Johnny Lee Smith of Winnie, Texas.

Inquiries should be addressed to:
Robert Kahla
P.O. Box 134
Stowell, Texas 77661

Published by: Cracked Egg Brand Press
P.O. Box 134
Stowell, Texas 77661

Illustrations: Cowboy Bob Kahla and Johnny Smith

ISBN Number: 1-882820-01-0

Printed By
D. Armstrong Co., Inc.
Houston, Texas 77092

CONTENTS

INTRODUCTION

Bob Kahla is a fourth generation cowboy from South East Texas. He grew up on a ranch where his father had a rodeo string, so riding broncs and bulls came naturally.

Bob was on the rodeo team at Sam Houston University where he earned a BS degree in animal science. He qualified for the National Inter-collegiate Rodeo Association National Finals in 1970 and 1971. He placed fourth in the nation in 1971 at Saddle Bronc riding.

Bob is now a horse trainer in Stowell, Texas. He is a member of the First United Methodist Church where he sings in the choir and teaches Sunday School. He enjoys being a role model for children. His poetry and songs demonstrate that a tough cowboy can be literate and sensitive.

**Bob Kahla & Freckle's Dixie Doll,
Fort Worth, Texas**

Bob Kahla Cowboy Poet
performing at
The Rice Festival

WHAT IT TAKES TO BE A COWBOY

What it takes to be a cowboy
Ain't a pair of faded jeans
Or a dusty hat or cowboy boots
All busted at the seams.

It ain't his looks or what he wears.
It's in his heart and mind.
His manners they are gracious
And his ways are mostly kind.

His smile is quick. His voice is soft.
He has a gentle way
With children and with animals
He meets along life's way.

He tips his hat or gives a nod
To ladies that he meets.
An outstretched hand he offers
To each gentleman he greets.

He's firm in his convictions.
He's quick to lend a hand.
With justice and with righteousness
He always takes a stand.

To those about in need of help,
His hand is never slow.
He never boasts. He never brags.
He never makes a show.

To think of life without him
Would make me very sad.
The reason is because you see
This cowboy is my dad.

The End.

"My Dad" Bill Kahla, 1947
in front of Kahla Hotel, a boarding house

Bob Kahla and Shorty

White's Ranch was established in 1818 and is the oldest Ranch in Texas. It was once the largest ranch in the state and is still owned by the Whites.

I break horses for this Ranch which inspired me to write this poem about the old days. The Crossed W, their brand, is not only a brand for cattle but a symbol of ranching tradition.

LEADING HORSES FOR WHITE'S RANCH

I'uz ridin broncs for the W crossed.
'Tween me and them weren't no love lost.
I wasn't fond of them
And they most surely musta hated me.

I knew they did by the way they'd fight
And buck and beller with all their might
And fill my life
with pain and misery.

I caught this snake one summer day
and started out to earn my pay.
To think a cowboy's
What I thought I'd wanta be.

Them was the days of the loin disease
And the cows would chew up bones and trees
And anything else
They thought might give 'em ease.

I roped this cow with a bone in her mouth.
I laid a trip and I headed south.
I'll tell you how
That outlaw broke an egg in me.

We stretched the twine, and we laid her down,
And fore my foot near hit the ground,
He broke in two
And went as high as any horse could ever be.

Well, he bucked and he bellered
and he swallered his head.
I thought, oh no! This time I'm dead.
Salt grass marsh and gator holes
as far as my two weary eyes could see.

Well, I landed face first on the ground,
Right by a big ole muskrat mound.
By now the taste
Of mud and dirt was nothin' new to me.

When I come to and begin to talk,
I told that bronc for that you'll walk;
Back to White's Ranch,
You'll walk, you wait and see.

Well, I led that horse ten miles that day.
I guess I really made him pay.
I showed that bronc,
There ain't no horse could get the best of me.

Bob Kahla & Peppy's Cuatro

That's me, Bob Kahla, and Peppy in a standoff with a cow

The **O** or **Mashed O** is the Brand of the McFaddin's Ranch, once a huge Ranch in Southeast Texas. Breaking horses on McFaddin's Ranch inspired this poem, Troubles on the Mashed O.

I was breaking horses on that ranch when I met a cowboy named Lester Jackson. Lester told me some great stories. He told me about when he first went to work for that ranch.

Kennith Day, The Big Smoke, he called him, said, "Boy, you'll have to learn to get along with me and my horses!"

He said, he found out what he meant the first day. They roped a big dun horse for him and that horse couldn't buck him off so he just reached around and bit him on the leg — had to take his whip handle to make him turn loose — had to ride him all day.

He said, boys would come out from town and try to be cowboys, but the bad horses and mosquitos would send 'em packing.

Bob Kahla, West Monroe, LA - 1965
This is me "having fun"

TROUBLES ON THE MASHED O

Gather round boys
For my tale of woe,
And I'll tell you 'bout my troubles
On the ole Mashed O.

Tell you 'bout the horse
That changed my ways
And really put an end
To my wranglin days.

Down in the marsh
Where the bayou flows,
And the skeeters and the gators
And the salt grass grows

Was a line back dun,
Stood sixteen hands,
And there on his hip
Was the Mashed O brand.

Cold as a cotton mouth,
Lean as a wolf,
Meanest ole critter
Ever walked on a hoof.

Hide full of ugly
And chuck full of mean,
Was the rankest ole bronc
That I ever had seen.

Well, the boss steps up,
And he says to me,
"On this outfit
Ain't nothin' free."

"You eat my chuck,
And you draw my pay;
You'll ride ole Dunny
'Til the end of the day."

All of a sudden
I yearn for the sound
Of the streets of the city
And the lights of the town.

A-hitten 'em high,
Down the trail I go.
I'm a-gettin' me gone
From the Ole Mashed O.

I sweeps pool halls
For my bed now.
There's no more a-chasin'
Of the Zebu cow.

Of a Cowboy's Life
I want no more.
Rather clean the John
And sweep the floor.

I have no need
For boots or hat
Or chaps or spurs
Or none of that.

I want no part,
No more, I know,
Of the broncs and the brehmers
On the Ole Mashed O.

9

Being a horse trainer I have to buy and sell horses, so I guess I'm a horse trader. Often an older cowboy will say, "I want to own just one more good horse. He'll be the last Caballo I'll ever have to own."

THE LAST CABALLO

He says to me, "I want a horse.
I want him young and strong.
Don't want him tall and leggy
Cause now my knees are gone."

He said, "I'll keep him fat and slick.
He'll have a decent home.
He'll be the last caballo
That I'll ever have to own."

He said, "the ones I used to ride,
Most of them are gone.
I used to ride a good'un though,
Just like that little roan."

The old cowhand, now had found a friend.
The roan had found a home.
He'll be the last caballo
That he'll ever have to own.

Next morning when they found him,
They knew that he'd been thrown,
Cause grazing there beside him
Was that stocky little roan.

Some folks may pause and ponder
Why it's written on his stone:
"That was the last caballo
That he'll ever have to own."

© 1991 Bob Kahla

Uncle Gene and Brown Jug

Grandpa Louie
Grandma Matile
&
Waye Hargraves
1943

Pa Louie
and
Frenchy

TV COWBOY

He rides a hoss and packs a gun,
But we all know it's all in fun
Cause he ain't never shot no one.
He's just a TV cowboy.

He wears a little piece of hair
Upon his head, for it is bare.
Why heck, he's slick from here to there.
He's just a TV cowboy.

It's make-up and them skin tight jeans,
It's them what makes him look so mean.
We see him on the little screen.
He's just a TV cowboy.

He always wears a padded shirt,
And girdle does his middle girt.
Why heck, he's just a little squirt.
He's just a TV cowboy.

It's four inch lifts and fake mustache
And his breath, it smells like day-old hash,
But man, he's really got the cash.
He's just a TV cowboy.

The End.

Growing up My Heros were TV Cowboys, Singing Cowboys.
So I wrote a poem poking fun at my heros, the TV cowboy.

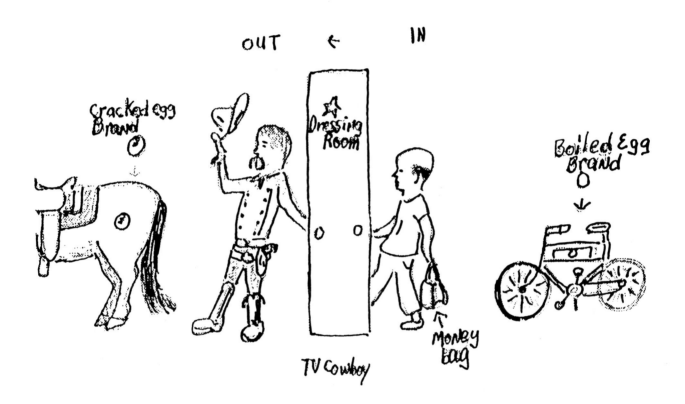

Uncle Eugene had a horse called Jesse James. He was gentle to saddle and handle but was almost impossible to ride. He would buck and whirl. The Heberts of Hebert's Ranch loved to borrow him to fool people into trying to ride him. They would tell an unwary stranger "Papa rides that horse." If the stranger tried to ride that horse he was surely thrown and the Hebert boys would fall off the fence laughing. Then one day a cowboy rode up. His name was Pete Sells. The Heberts fooled him into riding that horse. They said, "Papa rides him." Well, Pete rode him and he rode him so easily that he even 'fanned' him with his hat. When he was done and he got down, he said, "I don't know who Papa is, but if he rides that ole horse he must be a bronc riding ole sun-of-a-gun."

PAPA RIDES HIM

On cow outfits where I come from,
The pranks and jokes were sure to come,
To anyone who ventured by,
And thought he'd stick around and try

To make a hand and make a day
A-punchin' cows to earn his pay.
We had a horse named Jesse James,
But sometimes called him other names.

He'd stand so good. He wouldn't fight.
He'd let you pull the saddle tight.
But if a cowboy took a dare
And climbed aboard, he'd hit the air.

And buck and bawl to beat the band
And leave him sitting in the sand,
A-thinkin' of new ways to say
The names he'd made for him that day.

And if a stranger came around,
'Specially if he came from town,
We'd smile and lie to him and say
Our papa rides that little bay.

And if the stranger took the bait,
We'd stand around and watch and wait
And laugh until we'd nearly bust,
To see him laying in the dust.

Then one day a hand rode up
And we could tell he weren't no pup.
His boots was high. His brim was wide.
He wore a six gun at his side.

His hands were tough, His legs were bowed,
Was many broncs since he'd been throwed.
But still we thought our little bay
could get the best of him that day.

We snickered as we told him lies;
How, "that's the one our papa rides."
Up to that bronc that stranger strode.
Across his back his kack he throwed.

He cinched him up and went astride
And settled in that bronc to ride.
That outlaw squalled and hit the sky
And landed hard, kickin' high.

Still on his back that twister sat
And even fanned him with his hat.
That horse would twist and leave the ground
And try to shake that rider down.

He'd double back to where he'd been
'Til we thought that he would lose his skin.
That stranger sat there all the while,
And through the dust we saw a smile.

And when the dust was cleared and gone,
And we could tell who'd finally won,
Our hoots and hollers died away.
That stranger rode our horse that day.

He caught his horse, then turned to go,
Then turned around and said, "You know,
Now, I ain't met your papa yet,
But if he rides that bronc, I bet

He could ride 'em in his time.
I wish I'd known him in his prime,
'Cause, if he rides that horse for fun,
He must be a bronc riding ole son-of-a-gun."

COWBOYS ARE 'SPOSE TO BE TOUGH

I know that us cowboys
Are 'spose to be tough
And never do house work
And dishes and stuff.

We're 'spose to ride horses
And drive them big rigs,
But if I don't help her,
She calls me a pig.

If I don't do dishes,
The laundry, the floors,
If I don't clean toilets
And help with the chores;

Then she just might leave me,
Then where would I be,
With no one to cook for,
Or clean for but me?

More likely the doghouse
Is where I'd abide,
A-scratchin' the fleas
As they crawled up my hide.

And fightin' ole rover
For scraps and a bone,
With only that dog
Between me and alone.

So boys you can rib me
And treat me unkind,
Hurrah me and mock me.
I really don't mind.

Cause helping her out
Is the least I can do,
After all that she does here
For me and my crew.

Me and the kids, here,
We know where we stand,
With kisses and kindness
And love that is grand.

She works hard all week
And she cooks and she cleans
And still through it all son,
She looks like a queen.

So boys, you can laugh,
You can call me some names,
But here with my sweetheart
Is where I'll remain.

A-working together
Through love and through life,
And thank God in heaven
For making my wife.

One Sunday, after church, my wife and I were sitting around the house.
She wanted to clean house and I wanted to take a nap.
So after I got through washing dishes, I wrote this poem.

"My Wife" Evette on her horse Tarisito
(Note the Tennis shoes)

Bob, Evette, Terri, Shelly & Luke

My Dad, Bill
& his little brother Gene
1927

"Me" on my Cowhorse, Shorty
1956

Best Friends
My Dad, Rabbit Rowland, Uncle Gene and Duke Gill

18

THE DAYS OF MY YOUTH

Son, I recall now
The days of my youth,
Back before I got
So long in the tooth

And big in the middle
And gray in the hair.
Come sit down beside me,
My story I'll share,

Of days when I rode
For the Half Circle M;
Where the living was fine,
But the wages was slim.

The hours were long
And the work it was hard,
But the worries were few
And we went to bed tired

And woke up next morning
Just feeling so fine,
You'd a-thought that our coffee
Was souped up with wine.

A-workin' the cows
And a-feeding the stock,
We never had need
For a watch or a clock.

Then my ambition
And I had a row.
My ambition won.
Would you look at me now,

A-sittin' up here
In a suit and a tie,
In a cubby hole office
Up next to the sky.

I live in a penthouse.
I eat the best fare.
My car has a chauffeur
Who treats it with care.

I have all the things
that I wanted so bad,
So why the heck
Am I feeling so sad;

So downright regretful
And lonesome and blue?
My friends tried to tell me
But I thought I knew.

If I could just turn back
The time just a tad,
Back toward my youth son,
When I was a lad,

I'd trade in these ulcers
And headaches and stress,
The bills and the worries
That go with this mess,

And high tail it back
To the Half Circle M;
Where the living was fine,
But the wages were slim.

In the old days we used to drive cattle up from the salt grass in the spring. The young cowboys would have to herd the cattle on the beach all night until daylight, then move 'em North. That's what inspired this poem, "My Horse And I Now See The Sun."

MY HORSE AND I NOW SEE THE SUN

My horse and I now see the sun
Inching up the sky.
We hear the gull and wonder how
It'd be if we could fly.

We gallop through the briny surf
And out across the sand
And wonder how our tiny lives
Fit our masters plan.

We wonder at the auburn sky
And clouds of pink and white.
Now, as we rush to meet the day,
We're bathed in morning light.

The End.

©1991 Bob Kahla

Cousin Vernon's Honky Tonk after a storm in 1942

**This picture was taken at Gilcrest Bolivar Peninsula
while bringing cattle out of the Saltgrass.**

Uncle Joe Altman with truck and trailer

MY DOG CAN DO HIS JOB SO WELL

My dog can do his job so well.

He jumps around and wags his tail.

He yips and yaps and barks aloud.

His dance would make a mother proud.

He knows I'm home before I'm there,

And smiles to greet my weary stare.

His job is just to cheer me up,

And when I see the little pup,

I kneel and hug him in my arms

And know I'm home now safe from harm,

And I thank the one who's up above

For sending me this pup to love.

A friend who gives me all he's got,

And in return he asks for naught,

Just that his simple needs are met,

And sometimes take him to the vet.

It's food and water every day,

And pats and hugs and sometimes play.

I give him shelter from the cold,

Soft food when he is growing old.

Now, there's a tear drop in my eye.

I have to tell my friend goodbye.

Goodbye my friend, you were the best.

I hope you have a gentle rest.

Uncle Gene and cowdog pups, Rex and Tex

Pa Louie with his Dun Mare
1928

Back when I was rodeoing, riding saddle broncs and bareback horses, Bobby Stiener called me and said that they were short of saddle bronc and bareback riders for their rodeo at Belton, Texas. It being 'Rodeo Christmas', the Fourth of July, there were so many rodeos going on that there were not enough cowboys to go around.

Bobby said if I would enter both events, he would pay my entry fees. So I went to Belton and drew the 'Bucking Horse of the Year' in the bareback. Well, he bucked me off so hard, the very first jump, that the gate man said, "Git up, boy, and let us shut the gate." I got up and grinned and went behind the chutes and 'like ta' cried.

So I wrote a poem about 'Rodeo Christmas' at Belton, the Fourth of July.

Bob Kahla at Astrodome on Silver Tip
1974

RODEO CHRISTMAS THE FOURTH OF JULY

It was a Rodeo Christmas, the Fourth of July
When Bobby, he called me and said with a sigh,
"We're short of bronc riders at Belton again,
If you will just enter I know that you'll win,
And also the bareback, we need quite a few,
There's not many entered, I think maybe two.
Your fees I will pay, and a steak I will buy,
If you'll just work Belton, the Fourth of July."

Well, Belton it is then, I said with a grin,
If you'll throw in a room at the Holiday Inn.
He said, "That's too steep, but I'm sure in a fix,
I'll get you a room down at ole Motel Six."
I told him I'd be there, it'd sure be a breeze,
To not have to work stock to pay up my fees.
I hung up the phone without saying good-bye,
Now, I'd be at Belton, the Fourth of July.

I pulled down my hat, and I hit for the door,
A-grabbin' my saddle and bag from the floor.
Three hundred miles wadn't much of a drive,
If I held it to ninety, I could make it by five.
I jumped in my heap, the 'battry' was numb.
It was out on the highway a-ridin' my thumb.
If I could just flag down some cars passing by,
Then I could make Belton, the Fourth of July.

I limped into town, got a room with a view,
Then down to the 'rena' to see what I drew.
There on the pen fence, hung on a nail,
Was the draw of the day.— My skin it turned pale,
My eyes was a-bulgin', my blood pressure dropped.
At the sight of that number, my heart nearly stopped.
Oh, no, I'm doomed, I moaned a low cry,
I should'a worked Pecos, the Fourth of July.

Ole Widow Maker was number thirteen,
As bad as a grizzly and as big and as mean.
He run in the chute and he kicked and he roared.
And the top of his back was above the top board.
The bronc in the chute, that filled me with fear
Was voted by cowboys, the 'Bronc of the Year.'
And I had to ride him, at least I would try,
Down there at Belton, the Fourth of July.

I let out my riggin' as far as it would,
Then cinched it down on him the best that I could.
I took a deep seat upon his broad back,
And called for the gate with my feet in the cracks.
I marked him out good way up in the neck,
And that's when, I tell ya', all things went to heck.
We were a-headed for up in the sky,
Right there at Belton, the Fourth of July.

He leaped from the chute, he left like a jet.
He tore out my 'hand-holt', but wadn't through yet.
He jumped in the air and he kicked out behind.
I landed head first and I thought I'd gone blind.
I lay there in darkness and pondered my fate.
I heard someone holler, "We can't shut the gate."
Crumpled and blinded, in the gate I did lie,
At dusty ole Belton, the Fourth of July.

"If some of you boys will give me a hand,
We'll pull this poor cowboy's head from the sand."
They pulled at my arms and tugged at my shirt,
And I could see light as my head left the dirt.
Well, I sold off my riggin' and sold out my tack,
And I cut a trail and I never looked back.
Now, I may go blind as time passes by,
But it won't be at Belton, the Fourth of July.

A COWBOY PONDERED CHRISTMAS

A cowboy pondered Christmas
As he sat there in the mall.
His hand on his life savings
That he'd earned back in the Fall.

His pa would get a pair of gloves,
His ma a can of snuff
And if there was a little left,
He'd get himself some stuff.

He knew he'd need a pair of socks,
His other pair was old.
He hoped St. Nick would think of him
Before it got real cold.

Twenty bucks was not a lot,
But when he'd add the rest,
He bowed his head and thanked the Lord,
For he knew that he'd been blessed,

With mornings on the prairie
When dew was on the grass
Or sunsets in the evening
With the day a-fading fast.

With birds a-singing; "Morning Sir,
Now let this day begin."
With time to be out on his own
And time to be with friends.

He thanked the Lord for giving him
A horse to ride each day,
And cowwork in the spring and fall,
A chance to earn his pay.

With fencing in the summer time,
The sun a-bearing down,
And feeding in the winter time
And haying on the ground.

A new born calf with knobby knees,
A cold and frosty morn.
He thanked the Lord for blessin' him,
The day that he was born.

For he was born a cowboy
And a cowboy all the way,
Though he'd had to work at other things
To keep the wolf away.

Like the time he drove that truck,
But still, he wore his boots.
Or that time he worked in town
And had to wear them suits.

But still, he was a cowboy
And his thoughts were of the range,
a-riding and a-roping,
Now his life he would not change.

For Christmas time to cowboys
Is a time to be with God,
To tip his hat to heaven
And to give the stars a nod,

And thank the Lord for sending down
His Son to save us all.
That cowboy pondered Christmas
As he sat there in the mall.

26

A Cowboy Powdered Christmas

SIDE SADDLE SLIM

The name it was Side Saddle Slim.
The hair it could use a good trim.
This cowpoke would ride
And sit on the side.
Now was he a her or him?

Unknown Cowhand sitting side-saddle

The
Cracked Egg
Brand

Side-saddle Slim

DEW AND KHAKI
(A poem about imaginary friends)

Some friends of mine asked me to go
Out on a cattle drive.
I asked my mom and she said, "Sure."
Why heck, I'm almost five!

My mom pretends to see them,
And she knows their names so well.
They know my mom can't see them,
But they're too nice to tell.

For they are my friends only
And NO ONE else can see
Or hear their little voices
When they're playing there with me.

We climbed aboard my hobby horse
And rode around the drive.
I always have to take the reins.
Why heck, I'm almost five!

Their names are Dew and Khaki.
Did I forget to say?
Any time I think of them
They're there as plain as day.

But my eyes only see them
And when Mom tells me good night;
I say a prayer of thanks for them
When Mom turns out the light.

The End

Bobbie Platt Kahla

**My Momma Bobbie
in front of Freyburg Methodist Church**

**My Daughter Terri
and her hobby horse
1974**

THE ROUND UP

If Jesus is a shepherd
Could He be a buckaroo?
Could He ride the range and rope and sing
The way the cowboys do?

If Jesus was my saddle pal,
Oh, how my life I'd change.
I'd never tell another lie
Or take His name in vain.

I'd never cheat again at cards
Or drink or fight or cuss.
I'd turn the cheek as Jesus did
And never make a fuss.

But friend, the Lord is with us
As we speak, I tell you true.
If you believe and call to Him,
He's there to answer you.

So from now on, just live your life
As if the Lord were there.
And He could hear your every word
And know your every care.

If we believe in Jesus and
Repent our sins and all
Then we might ride with Jesus
In His round up in the fall.

I wrote this poem for my church, The First United Methodist Church
of Winnie, where I sing in the choir and teach Sunday School.

Herd of Cattle in Saltgrass

A Good ruN beats a 'pore' staNd

Buck Hamilton and I were feeding the stock after a rodeo and, being teenagers, we were anxious to get through with work and find some fun. That night a local man kept trying to rope the calves, keeping us from feeding. Well, Buck says in his toughest voice, "Get out of the pen." That man got so mad, he jumped off his horse and grabbed Buck by the shirt. Well, Buck hit him so hard that he did a pinwheel in the air before he hit the ground.

My friend knocked that 'local' down eight times and he got up eight times. So young Buck ran for the fence and I hollered, "What are you gonna do, get a cedar post and make him stay down?" He said, "No, I've had enough, I'm leaving!"

So that's what inspired this poem —

34

A GOOD RUN BEATS A POOR STAND

At the rodeo dance last Saturday night,
Ole Smokey Joe had an itch to fight.
But we thought he musta lost his goods
When he picked a fight with Bully Woods.

Joe gave ole Bull a shove or two
And all of us that knew Bull knew,
It didn't take that much provokin'
To get Bull riled, ole Bull was smokin'.

Ole Bull, he roared and run at Joe.
It was round-and-round and do-si-do,
Joe hit him hard, right on the chin.
Bull shook it off and laughed and grinned.

Now Joe could tell what we all knew;
He'd bit off more than he could chew.
Well, Joe had fought the Golden Gloves,
But Bull was kick and bite and shove.

If Bull could get one hairy fist
Upon Joe's neck, he'd give a twist.
It'd be lights out for Joe that night.
He'd never start another fight.

Ole Bull could never hit Joe none.
Joe'd dance around and hit and run.
Joe musta hit him forty times,
But still he never rang Bull's chimes.

Then Joe hit Bully one time more
Then turned around and hit the door.
We stepped outside to watch him run.
I guess he figured that's no fun,

To hit a brute between the eyes
And watch him laugh instead of cry.
He was makin' tracks. He was sifting sand.
A darn good run beats a poor stand.

Well, I've rodeoed and been around,
This ain't my first trip here to town,
And boys, I've seen a fight or two
And maybe even had a few.

But that's my first time, there that night,
To see the loser win the fight,
And win the fight and clear the place
By beating fists up with his face.

The End.

That's me at San Antone', 1973

NOW WE'RE SHORT A TOP HAND

Lord, you know that cowboy
That you called the other night?
His outer shell was tarnished,
But his soul was pure and white.

We know he had his faults, Lord,
Like all us mortals do.
But, Lord, he always did his part,
And he was cowboy through & through.

We'd never doubt your wisdom, Lord,
We'd never doubt your will.
It's just that now we're short a top hand
Back here on our little hill.

We don't begrudge him heaven, Lord,
We know he earned his place.
It's just that now we miss his voice
And long to see his face.

It's not that we're not happy,
Cause he earned his just reward.
It's just that holdin' things together here
Is gettin kinda hard.

Lord, we sure do miss him
Back here on our little spread.
He'd always take the dirty jobs,
The ones that others dread.

And even when his back was bent
From toiling on life's road,
His cheerful smile and gentle voice
Would lighten up our load.

So, Lord, will you forgive us
If we whimper now and then?
It's not that we're not grateful
For the blessings that you send.

It's just that losing him
Was sure a lot to lose.
There's not another cowhand
That can ever fill his shoes.

We'd never doubt your wisdom, Lord.
We'd never doubt your will.
It's just that now we're short a top hand
Back here on our little hill.

Amen.

My Dad, Bill Kahla, 1947, the year I was born
Photo was taken on the beach

Black Devil at A&M. Who's the rider?
1955

Practice at home
1979

TO RIDE THE RANGE & ROPE AND SING
THE WAY THE COWBOYS DO

"To ride the range and rope and sing the way the cowboys do." This line from one of Bob Kahla's poems tells what Bob, a fourth generation cowboy, lives for.

Bob grew up in a ranching family. His great-grandfather was a German immigrant who ran cattle on the upper Texas gulf coast. In addition to being a ship captain, operating a sailing cargo boat on the bays around Galveston, the elder Kahla had a herd of about fifteen hundred head of common cattle, (longhorns) even after losing two herds in the great hurricanes of 1900 and 1915.

Louis Kahla, Bob's grandfather, grew up roping wild cattle and riding wild horses. Louis said if his father caught his boys "pulling leather" while riding a bucking horse, the tough old German would ride up and whip their hands off the saddle horn with his quirt. Pa Louie, as he was called in his later years, was working cattle and riding the prairie for the Cade Estate when he met his cajun wife to be, Matile. Cade's pasture ranged some sixty miles from Port Bolivia to Fannett. Louis and his bothers would sometimes ride their horses the sixty miles to Fannett to dance with Matile and her sisters.

There was little chance that Bob would grow up to be anything but a cowboy. His father, Bill, was a rancher. Bill also had an RCA Rodeo string, producing rodeos as far away as Georgia and Florida. Bob's father was a fine horseman who was way ahead of his time as a horse trainer in Southeast Texas where they still did things the "old ways." For example, the horses were allowed to run wild until they were four or five years old, then they were roped and tied up until their "heads got sore!" They were made to buck in a pen to get the "jump out of 'em"! Then it was outside until they were run down.

Bill preferred the gentler approach. He would use patience and a gentle hand to gentle break the many horses he broke and trained for ranch work. He was especially adept at teaching a horse to handle or "neck rein."

Bob's mother taught first grade for many years and read poetry to Bob when he was young. That probably helped instill in him his love of poetry.

Bob, or "Mr. Bob," that's what the kids call him, has been training horses full time on his family ranch headquarters. Kahla trains horses for cutting, reining, roping and ranch work, and anything else a horse can do. He has even trained a few mules.

Kahla also writes poetry in his spare time which is sometimes seldom as anyone who works with livestock knows. He also speaks in church were he sings in the choir and teaches Sunday School to the Junior High and High School kids.

SOME PEOPLE SAY
ALL THE COWBOYS ARE GONE

Some people say all the cowboys are gone,
The west is now tame; but they are all wrong,
For deep in my heart I still hear their song.
I show it so others will know it.

Now Popeye don't have to be out on the sea,
A-ridin' the waves for a sailor to be.
He's still an old salt, and a sailor he be.
He shows it so others will know it.

So Christians we are and Christians we'll be,
A-riding the range or out on the sea.
Our Lord will be with us wherever we be,
So show it so others will know it!

©1991 Bob Kahla

**Great Grandpa
Charles William Kahla
Born 1847**

**Pa Pa Louie Kahla
Born 1883**

"Ridin' drag"

42

SOME STORIES I'VE HEARD

A steam engine pulled it's train of cars out of the siding at Stowell, a little town between Beaumont and Galveston on the Gulf and Interstate Railroad.

A goodly crowd had gathered to meet the train, as was the custom in those days. That was back when cars were rarely seen and the train brought the mail, travelers, freight and news.

A raw boned, long legged cowboy on a little salt grass prairie pony appeared out of nowhere. He rode straight up to the smokestack of the steam engine and roped it with forty-five feet of grass rope, then set his horse down to break the rope. His hard twist line was not dallied, but tied hard and fast, as was the habit of Southeast Texas cowhands. The theory was, if his horse got jerked down, the brute that he had roped could not drag the downed horse fast enough to catch the grounded cowboy.

Dennie Gallier had broken many ropes as he and his brother would back their horses up tail to tail, tie their saddle ropes together, then ride full speed in opposite directions to see which would give first; rope, saddle, horse or man.

Well, Dennie had not accounted for the upward pull of the smoke stack on his hemp cord and as the crowd gasped, his horse was nearly dragged into the drive wheels, before the twine finally broke.

While Bill Picket, the famous black cowboy, was the first man to bulldog a steer, Dennie Gallier was the first in Southeast Texas and he did it off the fender of a car. A makeshift arena was made of cars and wagons and in that big corral the wild cowboy leaped from the fender onto the horns of the running ox. He then positioned himself so that he could bite the lip of the speeding bovine, then set down hard, flipping the steer bulldog style.

Gallier once roped an alligator from horseback. The snared gator began thrashing around, rolling up in the rope 'till he reached the saddle that the cowboy had just vacated.

Another time while driving cattle through the deep marsh where the mud and water often came up to the saddle skirts, Dennie's little salt grass prairie pony played out (became too tired to move and sulled or layed down). Not having a fresh horse, a bull was roped and thrown down for Dennie to ride, so rather than walk and carry his saddle, Gallier rode the bull out of the marsh—no bridle—they just drove the bull with his strange cargo along with the cattle.

When I was seven years old, my daddy, Bill Kahla, put on a rodeo at Galveston. Daddy had a ferocious brahman bull—Black Devil was his name—never ridden, and he usually caught and roughed up any rider who tried to ride him. Thirteen was his number and he was coal black with big looping horns. A dangerous beast if there ever was one—mean clear through. A gate was left open and this black hide full of hate ended up on the street in Galveston, where he stared into the picture windows as shocked citizens stared back as if the glass could protect them. Finally, the bull wound up near a pile of large poles where Hoot Deaton managed to rope him and tie him to a big pole. A small gage chain was then lassoed onto his horns, then tied to my dad's old bobtail cattle truck, and he was led back to the arena. By the time they got there, he was leading like a well broke saddle horse.

44

The big zebu brahman had been purchased from Andrew Johnson of Port Bolivar, Texas. Mr. Johnson was a rancher and the Justice of the Peace of his precinct for as long as he wanted to hold that seat. His people had come from Sabine Pass and he would say that anybody that was worth anything was either from Port Bolivar or Sabine Pass. One of his kin, Brad Johnson, was a rancher from Sabine Pass who lived by his own rules. "Them Johnson boys were rough," was what Mr. Chris Gentz would say about Brad and his brother. Brad carried a rifle, and if he rode up on some people working cattle, most likely White Ranch or McFaddin Ranch hands, he might just cut out what he wanted and drive them off. Brad's reputation preceded him and no one would try to stop him.

His nephew, who's name was also Brad, stayed at my grandmother's boarding house for awhile. He said, one time, when he was helping his uncle work cows, a cowboy made the elder Brad mad, so he shot him down right there in the cow pens and when the other hand started to run, he shot him, too. Young Brad said that he asked his uncle why he had shot the other man. Brad told him, "Dead men don't carry no tales."

"In Jefferson County," said Forbes Davidson, "if you wanted a deputy to quit, just give him a warrant for Brad Johnson."

Well, the ranchers of that corner of Texas, tired of riding scared and losing cattle, hired a gunman from Kansas to kill Brad Johnson. The man from Kansas rode into Sabine Pass and asked the first citizen he met where he could find Brad Johnson. He was pointed to a man stepping out into the street. He stepped out and called Johnson's name, then shot and killed him and would not let anyone check to see if he was dead. When asked if he needed an escort out of town, he said, he didn't think that the man who killed Brad Johnson would need an escort.

My great grandfather bought 200 'pick cows' from the Johnsons, in 1900, for $12.50 a head to replace some of the 1500 head he had lost in the Great Hurricane. He said they were very civilized people, the Johnsons, and treated him very well.

One spring morning my dad was mowing the yard when James Burden came walking up leading a horse. James said he had contracted to break the horse, but could not ride him. Every single time he got on him, he was thrown. James offered to mow the grass if my dad would ride the bronky colt. My dad agreed and they traded places. James mowed the acre of yard with the push mower while my dad rode the horse. Daddy said he had the colt figured out, early on. Each time he would start to buck, Dad would holler, pull his head up and spur him. Pretty soon, he could make him quit bucking with just a shout.

James finally finished cutting the grass, wiped the sweat from his brow and thanked my dad profusely, then climbed on the horse, to be thrown almost immediately and pitched off onto the grass that he had labored so hard to cut.

In 1923, a man named Thibodeaux and his family lived in a house at Double Gum Island. Double Gum Island was a grove of trees Northwest of Winnie, Texas. On the prairie, a grove of trees on a sea of grass was called an island, as in Pine Island, Brush Island, or the oaks of High Island.

This bunch of trees lay in the free range pasture used by several ranchers including: Willy B. Blakely, Monroe White, Floyd Dugat, and O.C. Devillier, to name a few. If one of their cattle ventured onto the Island, it was shot, skinned, butchered and hauled off by wagon to be sold. If a cowboy got too close, looking for strays, he might have had to dodge a few bullets from Thibodeaux's rifle.

Dave Brown said that he was riding near Double Gum one day when Thibodeaux started clipping the branches around his head with rifle bullets. He said that, as he took off on his horse in a dead run, he came upon some real thick brush. When his horse ducked under a low limb, he jumped on top of the brush and ran for about a hundred yards then jumped back down on his horse.

These ranchers got together and sent for a Texas Ranger to stop the rustling and the fireworks.

Captain Graves Peeler got off the train and spent the night at a hotel in Winnie, then rode in a wagon out to Willie B. Blakely's place, which was within seeing distance of Double Gum.

Peeler watched the Island for six days, then a plan was devised. Nine cows were driven, by Floyd Dugat, into the grove of trees that made up Double Gum Island. A shot was heard and only eight cows came back out. Graves Peeler rode in and dismounted to watch. He saw the two sons of rustler Thibodeaux skinning the fresh kill. They had the cow on her back, between two corn rows.

Peeler stepped over into their row and called out. They ran for the house, hollering and ran under the porch. Their daddy, hearing all the commotion, stepped out of the front door with a rifle. The Ranger told him to drop his gun. Thibodeaux then fired, from the hip, piercing Ranger Peeler's ear with a bullet. Captain Graves Peeler then shot the man, killing him. Lucky thing that was the only bullet in the old man's gun—lucky for the ranger, that is.

Anyone who knew my daddy very well will recognize these stories I just told. He was a master story teller. Another great story teller was Otto Smith. He was also a horse trader and speaking of a roping horse would say, "This old pony is pretty good transportation to a calf and when you pitch that slack, he just dies off and that calf comes zipping back by you." About a cutting horse, "He can cut a rat out of a pack, put him in a hole and put his foot over it." That fits right in with the man, daddy said, who tried to jump Mud Bayou, got half way across and saw he wasn't gonna make it, so he fetched a mighty lunge and jumped back; or the man who rode, or said he rode, a bucking horse from Brush Island to the Spindletop Gulley (some ten miles) with five riders trying to pick his head up. So here's to the cowboys. May their stories forever be told.

**Great Gramma
Ellen Hampshire Kahla**

**Great Grandma & Grandpa
Dugat**

My Grandmother Matile in foreground

Speaking at a school

IF I WAS A KID IN SCHOOL

If I was a kid in school,
I would follow all the rules,
And I'd never be the cause of Teacher's tears.
Nothing like the days of old,
When I used to be so bold,
And there was only air between my ears.

Now I sadly rue the day;
That's when all I did was play,
And I never tried to study any books.
I really was a fool
To think I was so cool,
Now, I find I can't get by on just my looks.

It really is too bad,
And it kinda makes me sad
To see the waste of youth on those so young.
If I had my chance again,
I would be my teacher's friend,
And I'd study 'til that final bell was rung.

If I hadn't been a clown,
If I hadn't fooled around,
If work I hadn't always tried to shun;
Then I wouldn't be a jerk,
And I wouldn't have to work,
And now I could retire and have some fun.

Grandma Matile, Toots and Teacher
Mrs. Margaret Herndon

I SEE THE GEESE A-WINGING SOUTH

by Mister Bob

I see the geese a-winging south
And hear their haunting call,
And wonder how they know to fly
When summer turns to fall.

They're ever flying southward
As a nip is in the air
And never think of heading north
'Til snow is melting there.

Some folks, I know, are like the geese;
Their bones begin to ache
For warmer climes and sunny shores
To lay about and bake.

Just like the geese: they hit the air,
The roads, the rails, the sea,
And know that when that north wind blows,
It's south they gotta be.

The End.

Goose Hunters

Louie Kahla with a load of melons

Grand Pa with a mess of ducks

(left to right)
Unknown man, Charlie,
unknown child, Joe Altman,
Pa Louie, Gene and Daddy

The End.
(Uncle Gene's Jack)